# THE SEASONS OF
# ARNOLD'S APPLE TREE
## by GAIL GIBBONS

*Voyager Books*
*Harcourt Brace & Company   San Diego  New York  London*

# FOR ERIC

Requests for permission to make copies of any part of
the work should be mailed to: Permissions Department,
Harcourt Brace & Company, 6277 Sea Harbor Drive,
Orlando, Florida 32887-6777.

Voyager Books is a registered trademark of
Harcourt Brace & Company.

The Library of Congress has cataloged the hardcover
edition as follows:
Gibbons, Gail.
The seasons of Arnold's apple tree.
Summary: As the seasons pass, Arnold enjoys a variety
of activities as a result of his apple tree. Includes a
recipe for apple pie and a description of how an apple
cider press works.
[1. Seasons—Fiction. 2. Apple—Fiction.] I. Title.
PZ7.G33914Se  1984  [E]  84-4484
ISBN 0-15-271246-1   ISBN 0-15-271245-3 pb
Printed by South China Printing Co., Ltd., Hong Kong

M O Q R P N

Special thanks to Tim Copeland of Copeland & Sons,
of Bradford, Vermont, for his help on the cider press.

Printed in Hong Kong

Arnold climbs up high into the branches of the apple tree.
He can see far, far away in every direction.

This is Arnold's very own secret place. This is Arnold's apple tree.

Arnold's tree keeps him very busy all through the year.

It is spring.

Arnold watches the small buds grow on his apple tree.

Some of the buds develop into sweet-smelling apple blossoms.

HONEYBEE AND APPLE BLOSSOMS
The honeybee makes honey from nectar, the sweet juice found in flowers.

Carefully and quietly, Arnold watches bees collect nectar from the blossoms to make honey.

Arnold makes a swing for his apple tree.

He weaves an apple-blossom wreath and hangs it from a branch.

Arnold picks an armful of apple blossoms and brings it to his family.
They make a flower arrangement together.

It is summer.

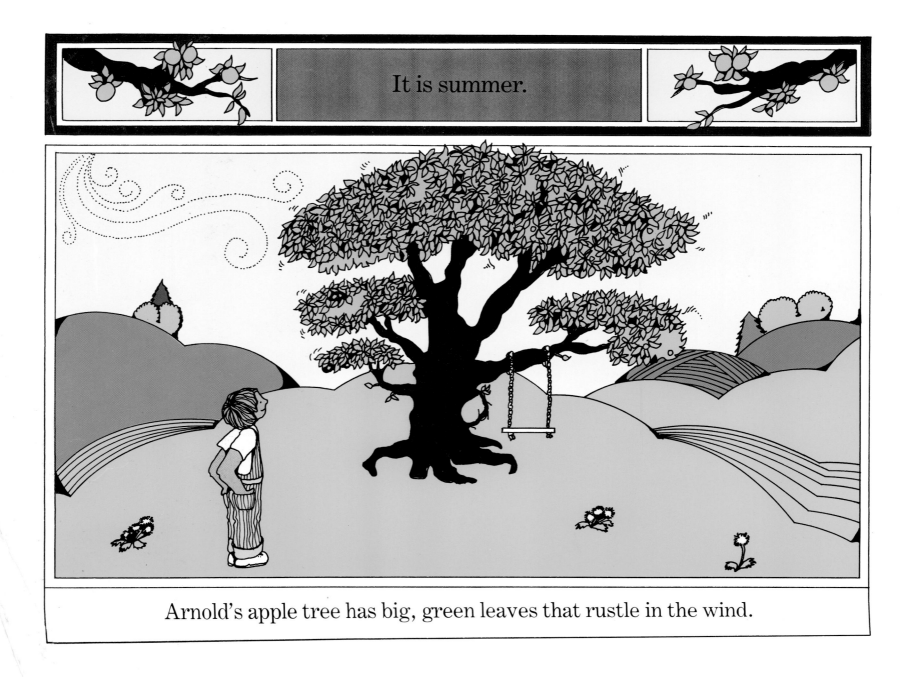

Arnold's apple tree has big, green leaves that rustle in the wind.

Arnold builds a tree house.

His apple tree shades him from the hot summer sun.

The green leaves shelter him during a summer shower.

Arnold watches small apples begin to grow from where the
blossoms used to be. They grow bigger, bigger . . .

and bigger.
With some of the big, green apples, Arnold does a juggling act
for his tree friend.

It is fall.

Arnold's apple tree now has big, red, tasty apples.

The green leaves have turned golden. They drift to the ground.

Arnold gathers some of the leaves and brings them up to his tree house to make a soft floor to lie on.

Arnold shakes the branches and red apples fall to the ground.
He puts them in a basket and takes them home.

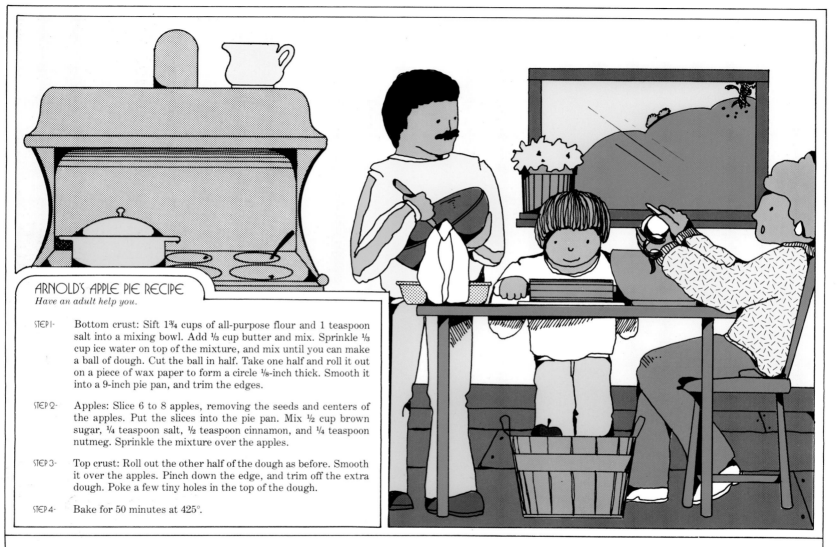

## ARNOLD'S APPLE PIE RECIPE
*Have an adult help you.*

STEP 1- Bottom crust: Sift 1¾ cups of all-purpose flour and 1 teaspoon salt into a mixing bowl. Add ⅓ cup butter and mix. Sprinkle ⅓ cup ice water on top of the mixture, and mix until you can make a ball of dough. Cut the ball in half. Take one half and roll it out on a piece of wax paper to form a circle ⅛-inch thick. Smooth it into a 9-inch pie pan, and trim the edges.

STEP 2- Apples: Slice 6 to 8 apples, removing the seeds and centers of the apples. Put the slices into the pie pan. Mix ½ cup brown sugar, ¼ teaspoon salt, ½ teaspoon cinnamon, and ¼ teaspoon nutmeg. Sprinkle the mixture over the apples.

STEP 3- Top crust: Roll out the other half of the dough as before. Smooth it over the apples. Pinch down the edge, and trim off the extra dough. Poke a few tiny holes in the top of the dough.

STEP 4- Bake for 50 minutes at 425°.

Arnold and his family make apple pies with apples from Arnold's apple tree.

## HOW AN APPLE CIDER PRESS WORKS

press screw handle

hopper

flywheel

press plug

tub

cloth filter

tray

1. Eight to ten apples are put into the hopper. When the flywheel is turned, blades inside the hopper chop the apples.

2. The apple pieces fall into the tub. Apples are chopped until the tub is three-fourths full.

3. The press plug is screwed onto the press screw. When the press screw handle is turned, the press plug squeezes the apple pieces and forces juice through the cloth filter.

4. The apple cider flows into the tray and drips into a container.

They put the rest of the apples into a cider press and make fresh apple cider.

On Halloween Day, Arnold decorates some of the biggest apples.

They glow in the moonlight under his tree on Halloween night.

It is winter.

Snow falls. It is quiet. The branches of Arnold's apple tree are bare.

Arnold hangs strings of popcorn and berries on them for the winter birds to eat.

He builds a snow fort around the bottom of his tree.

Arnold builds a snowman to keep him and his tree company during the winter.

The snow melts away.
It is spring again . . . .